The Merchant of Venice

William Shakespeare

RETOLD BY
TINA NARANG

SCHOLASTIC
New York Toronto London Auckland
Sydney New Delhi Hong Kong

Published by Scholastic India Pvt. Ltd.
A subsidiary of Scholastic Inc., New York, 10012 (USA).
Publishers since 1920, with international operations in Canada, Australia, New Zealand, the United Kingdom, India, and Hong Kong.

First edition: May 2012
Reprint: September 2018 February 2020 Dec 2023 Feb 2024

ISBN-13: 978-81-8477-089-6

Printed at Ram Printograph, Delhi

The Lexile measure of this book (1100L) represents the complexity of the text. This Lexile measure—along with other characteristics of the text, such as developmental level and subject matter—helps in selecting books that best match a reader's level and goals. For more information on using Lexile measures to connect readers with text, visit www.Lexile.com.

Contents

Characters

The Duke of Venice

The Prince of Morocco: *suitor to Portia*

The Prince of Arragon: *suitor to Portia*

Antonio: *a merchant of Venice*

Bassanio: *his friend*

Solanio: *friend to Antonio and Bassanio*

Salarino: *friend to Antonio and Bassanio*

Gratiano: *friend to Antonio and Bassanio*

Lorenzo: *in love with Jessica*

Shylock: *a Jewish moneylender*

Tubal: *a Jew, his friend*

Launcelot Gobbo: *a clown, servant to Shylock*

Old Gobbo: *father to Launcelot*

Leonardo: *servant to Bassanio*

Balthazar: *servant to Portia*

Stephano: *servant to Portia*

Portia: *a rich heiress*

Nerissa: *her waiting maid*

Jessica: *daughter to Shylock*

Magnificoes of Venice, officers of the Court of Justice

Gaoler, servants to Portia, and other attendants

1

Italy in the sixteenth century—a time when kings still ruled, men still wooed and fortunes still sunk at sea. The place—Venice—one of the richest in the world, where passions ran high—for love, for money, for religion and *even* for flesh. In this city of riches and of passions lived the princes, the dukes, the merchants, the rich heiresses and the moneylenders.

And since all stories must perforce begin with a 'once upon a time', so too does this one. Once upon a time there was a wealthy ship owner called Antonio, quite simply a merchant of Venice. Antonio had a prosperous business; his ships plied the seas with precious cargo of silks and spices, and he was considered one of the most honourable men in all of Venice, respected by all, and hated by none. Well, almost.

But sometimes even the best of men can be overcome by an unexplained sense of sadness. Like Antonio was. So here was a fortunate but cheerless man surrounded by friends, each attempting to lift his sagging spirits.

'Is it the fate of your ships?' asks Solanio, hopefully.

'Or perhaps it is love!' adds Salarino.

'Fie, fie!' says Antonio, dismissing them both.

Even Gratiano, believed to talk more than any other man in Venice and make less sense than most, cannot lift his spirits. As they stroll slowly along a street in Venice, this motley group is joined by some more friends, among them Bassanio, one of Antonio's closest friends.

When they all part ways a short while later, Bassanio, finally finding himself alone with Antonio, lays bare his soul to him, telling him that he loves Cato's daughter, Portia, who is a beautiful and virtuous woman and a rich heiress in Belmont. News of her beauty has spread far and wide and renowned suitors have tried to win her hand. But much as he would like to court Portia, Bassanio admits sadly that he lacks the means to do so. Antonio assures him that his purse and his person are at his friend's service and tells him that since all his money is at sea, he should try to get credit in his name in the city of Venice.

***

In another part of Italy too, there are young people who seem as weary of the world as Antonio! At Belmont, the beautiful Portia tells her waiting maid, Nerissa, that her frail form is weary of the world. She complains that she can neither choose who she likes nor refuse who she dislikes as she has to follow the will of her dead father. Nerissa tells

Portia to take comfort in the fact that her virtuous father devised the lottery of the three chests before his death with the best of intentions for his daughter's future.

The rules of the lottery were simple. Of the three chests—one of gold, the other of silver and the third of lead—only one carried the portrait of Portia. And only the suitor who chose the correct casket would get to marry Portia.

When quizzed by Nerissa on whether she sees any worth in the suitors that have courted her so far, Portia dismisses each one swiftly. Not for her the coltish Neapolitan prince who talks of nothing but his horse and whose mother probably flirted with a horse smith. Or the sad, frowning, melancholic County Palatine who was only likely to get worse with age. Not either the French lord, Monsieur Le Bon, who fences with his own shadow—marrying him would be like marrying twenty husbands, not one.

Not certainly Falconbridge, the young baron of England, with his dumb demeanour and odd clothes, who knew neither Latin, nor French, nor Italian, nor even English for that matter. Gone too was the baron's neighbour, the Duke of Saxony's nephew, who even at his best was worse than a man, and at his worst worse than a beast. And here lay the dilemma: Portia could not reject a suitor and go against her father's will, not even if he was as unlikeable as any of the above. If a suitor chose the right casket, she was sworn to accept the choice. And Portia is determined to follow her father's will, saying that she would rather live to be as old as Sibylla or die as chaste as Diana if her hand were not won in accordance with her father's will.

But no one has been suitable or unsuitable thus far. And no one has made a lasting impression. Except perhaps a certain gentleman called Bassanio. When Nerissa asks, 'Do you not remember, lady, in your father's time, a Venetian, a scholar and a soldier, that came here in the company of the Marquess of Monteferrat?

'Yes, yes, it was Bassanio; to the best of my recollection,' Portia replies.

'Of all the men that ever my foolish eyes looked upon, he was the best deserving a fair lady,' continues Nerissa.

'I remember him well, and I remember him being worthy of your praise.'

As they discuss suitors, a servant announces that four suitors wish to take leave of Portia and that a forerunner has come from the Prince of Morocco to announce that his master will be visiting Portia soon. Portia feels she has as little enthusiasm to welcome the fifth suitor as she has to bid the last four farewell.

***

In another part of Venice, a Jewish moneylender, Shylock, is having an intense conversation with Bassanio. Shylock does business at the Rialto, the financial and commercial centre of Venice.

'Three thousand ducats—well?' he asks.

'Ay, sir, for three months,' Bassanio confirms.

'For three months—well?'

'For which, as I told you, Antonio shall be bound.'

'Antonio shall become bound—well. Three thousand ducats for three months, and Antonio bound.'

'Your answer to that,' Bassanio asks.

'Antonio is a good man,' replies Shylock.

Shylock is clearly pleased. Three thousand ducats, for three months with Antonio as surety. But though he considers Antonio a good guarantor, Shylock does feel that his financial condition is precarious as all his ships are at sea, sailing to different places, whether it be Tripolis, the West Indies, Mexico, or England.

Nevertheless, seeing that Antonio is a worthy guarantor Shylock agrees to give Bassanio the loan of three thousand ducats. But there is a further condition: he wants some form of assurance from Antonio. 'I will be assured. May I speak with Antonio?' he asks. Bassanio invites him to join them for dinner so he can meet Antonio.

Shylock is a Jew with firm beliefs. A Jew who makes no attempt to hide his dislike for Christians, who claims that he will buy from Christians, sell to them, talk to them, walk with them but not eat, drink or pray with them. In short, a Jew who hates Christians like he does nothing else. So when Shylock spots Antonio, the very Christian merchant of

Venice, approaching them, all of Shylock's resentment and feelings of hatred come to the fore. He is resentful of many things, but most of all of Antonio's tendency to lend money, without too much emphasis on surety or guarantee, which brings down the general rate of interest for moneylenders in Venice. He believes that Antonio hates the race of moneylenders and resents the bargains and the mode of interest which moneylenders do business with.

But despite seething on the inside, Shylock greets Antonio with the words, 'Rest you fair, good signor, your worship was the last man in our mouths.' Antonio tells Shylock that he is not in favour of either lending or borrowing money; however, he is willing to make an exception for his friend, Bassanio, since he is in dire need of money. Shylock reconfirms the amount as three thousand ducats and Antonio confirms the period for the loan as three months. Shylock then asks Antonio what the bond or surety is likely to be.

Shylock prods him further by quoting the example of Jacob and his uncle Laban who made a deal that Jacob—who took care of his uncle's sheep so he could marry his daughter Rachel—got to keep all the striped and spotted animals that were born in his care. In order to profit from this arrangement, Jacob placed striped branches in front of the sheep when they mated, so the sheep would give birth to striped lambs. In this way Jacob soon became a rich man. Antonio thinks that Shylock has used a Biblical story to justify the practice of usury—lending money and charging interest—and feels that Jacob's success is an example of God's providence.

Antonio resents Shylock's use of Biblical references to his advantage. 'The devil can cite Scripture for his purpose,' he says. For Shylock seems to be a villain with an artificial smile, much like a good apple with a rotten core. Shylock repeats the deal to enquire about the rate of interest. He claims that Antonio has criticised him at the Rialto many a time, cursing his money and his business, all of which he has patiently tolerated, for suffering such accusations seems to be the bane of all moneylenders.

'Fair sir, you spit on me last Wednesday; you spurned me too; another time you called me a dog; and for these courtesies I'll lend you so much money? Since you call me a dog, let me ask you if a dog can lend three thousand ducats,' he asks sarcastically.

'I will call you a dog again, and spit on you too, and spurn you as well,' Antonio replies sharply.

Even as Shylock urges Bassanio and Antonio to go with him to a notary, Shylock states that there is a catch to the deal: if he is not repaid three months later to the day, he would take a pound of Antonio's flesh from whichever part of his body he wishes, as penalty. Antonio confirms, 'Yes, Shylock, I agree to this bond.' But Bassanio will have none of it. He says he would rather not take the money than agree to Antonio sealing such a dangerous bond. But Antonio assures him that he will not break the bond, as he expects to repay Shylock a month before the bond expires, for he is likely to earn three times the amount that he is borrowing.

Shylock jokes that he has nothing to gain by demanding this penalty as a pound of man's flesh is hardly as profitable as mutton or beef. Nonetheless, he urges Antonio to meet him at the Notary's where the bond can be prepared. He then goes in search of Tubal, a wealthy Jew, so he can arrange for the ducats, and also check on his house which he has left in the charge of a servant.

As Antonio bids Shylock farewell he cannot help make one last comment. 'This Jew might turn into a Christian owing to his kindness.'

'I do not like fair terms and a villain's mind,' Bassanio protests. But Antonio is confident that his ships will be home a month before the date on which the loan has to be repaid.

2

At Belmont, in Portia's house, there is yet another suitor. The dark-complexioned Prince of Morocco. The prince appeals to Portia not to be prejudiced against him on account of the colour of his skin for the strong colour has in fact won him the affection of many maidens. Portia assures him that her affections are not based on appearance but on the lottery her father has organised. A lottery that gives everyone a fair chance, whatever their appearance. Yet, he admits sadly, in the game of fortune, it is not always the better man that wins.

Reminding him of his oath—that if he chooses wrongly, he must never attempt to be her suitor again—Portia urges him to postpone his choice to after dinner. 'Good fortune then, to make me blessed or cursed among men,' the prince says as he leaves.

***

Meanwhile on a street in Venice, Shylock's servant, Launcelot Gobbo, is in a state of utter confusion, and cannot decide whether or not to leave the services of his Jewish master. Just then, his father, the blind Old Gobbo, comes by with a basket and asks him the way to Master Jew's house.

Launcelot recognises his father, and realising that he cannot see his own son because he is blind, decides to jest with him. He gives him madly confusing directions, 'Turn upon your right hand at the next turning, but, at the next turning of all, on your left; marry, at the very next turning, turn of no hand, but turn down indirectly to the Jew's house.' Obviously, Gobbo cannot make anything of these directions. So he asks Launcelot whether he knows if a certain Launcelot lives with the Jew. 'Are you asking about young Master Launcelot?' Launcelot teases. When Gobbo insists that the one he is looking for is a poor man's son and by no means a Master, Launcelot tells Gobbo that the young Launcelot has died and gone to heaven.

When Launcelot sees how distraught Gobbo is on hearing the news of his death, he asks his father if he recognises him. But Gobbo still cannot and requests Launcelot to tell him if his son is indeed alive or dead. 'I am sand-blind, and I do not know who you are,' he insists sadly. Launcelot then comments that even a father that can see may sometimes not know his own child, for it is a wise father that knows his own child.

By this time, Gobbo being a bit suspicious, asks Launcelot to stand up so he can make sure he is not his son. 'I am Launcelot, your boy that was, your son that is, your child that shall be.' Gobbo is not convinced. Launcelot insists that Gobbo is indeed his father as much as his wife, Margery, is his mother. When Gobbo reveals that he is carrying a present for Launcelot's master, Launcelot advises him to give the present to Bassanio instead, the master he wishes to serve now that he plans to leave his Jewish master, Shylock. Coincidentally, Bassanio walks by just at that moment.

'God bless your worship!' Gobbo says cheerily as father and son greet the unsuspecting Bassanio. Bassanio who is engaged in giving directions to a servant to have supper ready, deliver some letters, get the liveries prepared and summon Gratiano to his house, is completely bewildered.

'Oh mercy! What do you want from me?' he cries in alarm.

'Here's my son, sir, a poor boy … who has a great infection to serve …' says Gobbo.

'Indeed, the short and the long is, I serve the Jew, and have a desire—as my father shall specify …' adds Launcelot.

'I have here a dish of doves that I would like you to have; and my suit is …' Gobbo says with the utmost clarity.

'And what would your suit be?' demands Bassanio in exasperation.

To which Launcelot says simply, 'To serve you, sir.'

Bassanio welcomes the idea of Launcelot leaving a rich Jew's service to become the follower of a poor gentleman. He instructs a servant to give Launcelot a uniform so he can be dressed appropriately. Launcelot is pleased at his good fortune and beckons to his father. 'Father, come; I'll take my leave of the Jew in the twinkling of an eye.'

As Bassanio is instructing his servant, Leonardo, to take care of some urgent business, Gratiano comes by and requests Bassanio to take him to Belmont with him. 'You must not deny me; I must go with you to Belmont,' he insists.

'Why, then you must,' Bassanio says in return, but adds that he disapproves of his wild, rude and outspoken behaviour, which though not a fault among friends, may be wrongly interpreted by strangers. He requests Gratiano to exercise some restraint in his behaviour, so that it does not reflect on Bassanio and make him lose any chances he might otherwise have had.

***

At Shylock's house, in another part of Venice, Jessica is conversing with Launcelot in private and telling him that she is sorry to see him leave the service of her father. He did a lot to liven up her hellish house—she says sadly. Nevertheless she gives him a ducat as she bids him farewell. She also gives him a letter for Lorenzo since he is going to be meeting him at the dinner being hosted by Bassanio. Launcelot bids Jessica a tearful farewell saying that she has been a sweet Jew and that a Christian man will surely marry her.

Jessica is distressed that she should be ashamed to be her father's child, for she may be his daughter by blood, but she is not one by manners. 'O Lorenzo,' she sighs, 'if you keep your promise, I shall indeed become a Christian and your loving wife.'

***

Meanwhile, Lorenzo, Gratiano, Salarino and Solanio are preparing for the masquerade. While they are discussing their plans, Launcelot comes by with a letter for Lorenzo. Lorenzo recognises the fair hand that has written the letter. After delivering the letter Launcelot leaves to bid farewell to Shylock, his Jewish Master, so he can join the services of a Christian master that very night. Lorenzo tells Launcelot to assure Jessica in private that he will not fail her. Salarino, Solanio and Lorenzo decide to meet at Gratiano's house in an hour's time. Jesting that the letter he has just received must contain news of love, Gratiano asks Lorenzo if the letter is indeed from Jessica.

Lorenzo gives Gratiano Jessica's letter to read and reveals her plan to run away from her father's house dressed as a page boy and also her intention to carry gold and jewels with her. Jessica also plans to be Lorenzo's torch-bearer at the masquerade that night.

***

Shylock, in the meantime, is outside his house with Launcelot and complaining about Jessica, saying that his daughter wastes all her time sleeping, snoring and eating. When Jessica comes outside Shylock tells her that he plans to be out for supper and hands over his keys to her and requests her to look after the house in his absence.

Shylock is reluctant to leave the house as he feels his absence will lead to some misfortune. When Launcelot informs him that there is likely to be a masquerade that night, he is even more alarmed and asks Jessica to secure the house properly after he departs and be wary of revellers—the Christian fools in masques—on the street. He asks her to keep all doors and windows closed.

As Launcelot leaves the house to inform everybody that Shylock will join them for dinner, he whispers to Jessica under his breath, 'Mistress, look out of the window, for a Christian will come by who will be worth a Jewess' eye.' This does not escape Shylock's notice and he demands to know what he has said. Jessica replies plainly that Launcelot merely bid her farewell.

As Shylock leaves the house, he warns Jessica again, 'Do as I bid you—shut the doors after you.'

***

The masked Gratiano and Salarino eagerly await Lorenzo's arrival on the street near Shylock's house, and find it strange that a person in love should be running late. Aren't lovers supposed to be faster than time even? they wonder aloud.

A masked Lorenzo rushes in just then and claims

breathlessly that he was caught up taking care of certain affairs that needed urgent attention. They hurry towards Shylock's house. As they come close, Lorenzo tells them that it is the house of his future father-in-law, Shylock. Seeing them arrive, Jessica, emerges from the house, wearing boy's clothes. She asks Lorenzo to identify himself. Lorenzo says it is indeed him, 'Jessica's love.' Jessica asks whether he too loves her as much as she does him. Lorenzo tells her that he does indeed. 'Heaven and your thoughts are witness,' he adds.

Jessica hands over a casket full of jewels and tells Lorenzo that she is relieved he cannot see what ridiculous disguise she is in. 'You must look sweet, even in the guise of a boy,' says the lovelorn Lorenzo to Jessica. He tells Jessica to hurry up so they can make their way to Bassanio's feast without any further delay. Jessica quickly secures the house and returns with some ducats.

Just as Lorenzo, Jessica and Salerio are hurrying to the feast along with other masked revellers, Antonio catches up with them. He tells them that the masquerade is off. He informs them that several other developments have taken place, among which most importantly, Bassanio is preparing to set sail to take advantage of the strong wind that is blowing currently. Gratiano is delighted that they are going to sail the same night.

***

In Portia's house at Belmont, the Prince of Morocco is

finally ready to choose the casket. The prince approaches the caskets and reads out what each one says. The gold, which bears the inscription, 'Who chooses me shall gain what many men desire.' The silver that says, 'Who chooses me shall get as much as he deserves.' And the lead that warns, 'Who chooses me must give and risk all he has.'

'One of them contains my picture, Prince. If you choose that I am yours,' Portia adds.

The prince is utterly confused and considers each of the caskets, before he finally chooses the gold one. For it is only gold that befits someone like Portia, he says. The Prince of Morocco unlocks the golden casket and sees with shock what lies inside. The casket reveals a picture of rotting flesh, and a scroll that says:

All that glisters is not gold;
Often have you heard that told,
Many a man his life has sold,
But my outside to behold …
Your answer had not been inscrolled,
Fare you well: your suit is cold.

The prince exits sadly, bidding Portia farewell.

***

Elsewhere in Venice, it is rumoured that one of Antonio's ships might be in trouble, even as Bassanio sails out with Gratiano, setting sail before Shylock, accompanied by the Duke of Venice, could reach the ship and search for his missing daughter. When Shylock learns that Lorenzo and Jessica had been seen in a gondola, he displays a passion strange and outrageous. In fact it is difficult to say what pains him more, the loss of his daughter, or the loss of his ducats. 'My daughter!—O my ducats!—O my daughter! Fled with a Christian!—O my Christian ducats!' he shouts like a crazed man.

In the meantime, Salerio encounters a Frenchman who confirms to him that a ship is believed to have capsized in the English Channel—the narrow sea that divides England and France. Salerio fervently hopes that this ship does not belong to Antonio. Solanio advises him to break the news gently to Antonio. 'No gentleman kinder than him has ever walked the earth,' Salerio says of Antonio. He recounts to Solanio how when Antonio was parting from Bassanio he had told him to attend to his business and not worry about the Jew's bond, urging him to think chiefly of the courtship and the love it entailed. And then when tears had welled up in his eyes, he had turned his face and wrung Bassanio's hand in farewell. 'I think he only loves the world for him,' Solanio adds. They decide to go and seek out Antonio.

***

At Belmont, there is a steady stream of suitors, the latest being the Prince of Arragon. Portia directs the prince to the three caskets, telling him that if he chooses the one that contains her portrait they can be married right away, but if he fails then he must leave her presence immediately.

The prince recounts the three things he has sworn to—first, that he is never to reveal to anyone which casket he chose; second, if he fails to choose the right casket, he can never woo a woman for marriage, and lastly, if he is unlucky enough to not choose the right casket, then he must leave Portia and be gone from her sight forever. Portia assures him that all of her suitors have sworn to these conditions.

The prince then examines the three caskets, the first of gold, the second of silver and the third of lead, and reads aloud what each of them says. When he reaches the silver casket whose text proclaims, 'Who chooseth me shall get as much as he deserves,' the prince asks for the key.

As the prince turns the key an expectant silence fills the room. Arragon peers inside the casket to find a portrait of a blinking idiot holding a schedule that ends with the lines:

Take what wife you will to bed,

I will ever be your head:

So be gone, you are sped.

Soon after Arragon's departure, Balthazar informs Portia that there is a young Venetian at the gate, who wishes to announce the arrival of his master who has come bearing rich gifts much like an ambassador of love. Nerissa hopes that it is Bassanio.

3

There is a rumour doing the rounds at the Rialto that Antonio's ships are in trouble at sea, with one of them believed to have been shipwrecked at the Goodwins, a dangerously fatal place, where ships regularly capsize. Solanio and Salarino are walking along a street in Venice, discussing this news when they spot Shylock in the distance.

Going up to him, Solanio asks, 'How now, Shylock? What is the news among the merchants?'

Shylock replies that the biggest he has is of his daughter having run away. 'My own flesh and blood to rebel!' he says ruefully.

'Have you heard whether Antonio has had any loss at sea?' Salarino persists. Shylock replies that if Antonio has gone bankrupt, then he will need to check his bond. 'There I have another bad match: a bankrupt, a spendthrift, who scarcely shows his head on the Rialto … let him look to his bond … let him look to his bond,' he says threateningly.

'Why, I am sure, if he fails to return the money, you will

not take his flesh. What's that good for?' Salarino asks.

'To bait fish with, if it will feed nothing else, it will feed my revenge,' Shylock replies. He says that Antonio has disgraced and obstructed his business and dealings a great many times, and mocked his losses. And all because Shylock is a Jew.

'Does not a Jew have hands, organs, dimensions, senses, affections and passions like any other man?' he asks. 'Is he not fed by the same food, hurt with the same weapons, subject to the same diseases and cured by the same means, and warmed and cooled by the same winter and summer as a Christian is? If you prick us, do we not bleed? If you tickle us, do we not laugh? If you poison us, do we not die? And if you wrong us, shall we not revenge?' Even as Shylock continues, a servant comes by to summon Salarino and Solanio to his master Antonio's house as he wishes to speak with them both.

Shylock, in the meantime, still hoping to get news of his runaway daughter, meets up with Tubal and asks if he has any news from Genoa. Tubal reveals that he had come close to finding her several times but with no success. Shylock again moans the loss of the jewels that his daughter Jessica has carried with her. 'A diamond worth two thousand ducats in that, and other precious jewels,' he cries, and the losses are just mounting up, as he is also spending money to find her.

Tubal cuts in to remind him that other men are unlucky

too. Antonio for instance, whose ship has been wrecked on its way from Tripolis, news that has been confirmed by the sailors that escaped the mishap. When he hears this, Shylock cries out in delight, 'Good news, good news! Ha, ha!' Tubal adds that creditors say that Antonio has incurred huge losses through this loss at sea and is certain to become bankrupt.

'I am very glad of it; I'll plague him, I'll torture him; I am glad of it,' Shylock shouts in his excitement. He then asks Tubal to find him an officer who will check with Antonio a month before the bond period is up to see if he is likely to keep his word and repay the loan. He requests Tubal to meet him later at the synagogue.

***

At Belmont, Portia requests Bassanio to delay the task of choosing the caskets. 'I pray you, pause a day or two before you take the risk, for if you choose wrongly, I will lose your company.' She wishes she could tutor him to make the right choice. But she has been sworn to keep the true nature of each casket a secret. She feels torn between her feelings for him and her loyalty to the oath.

But Bassanio does not want to wait any longer. 'If you do love me, you will find me out,' Portia says hopefully, for a certain casket will indeed lock their fortunes together. She then asks for music and waits nervously to see how Bassanio will choose.

Bassanio surveys the three caskets. He decides to lighten

the atmosphere with some inane rhymes, so he chants, 'Let us all ring fancy's knell: I'll begin it—ding dong bell.' And everyone repeats after him, 'Ding dong bell.' Bassanio thinks there is a danger in going by outward appearances, so he decides to avoid the gold casket. He also does not go for the silver casket. Instead it is the lead casket that he picks, whose plain appearance threatens rather than promises anything. Bassanio is moved by its plainness. And with a flourish he proclaims, 'And here choose I: let the result be a happy one!'

Without further delay, Bassanio opens the casket and finds a portrait of Portia inside. He praises the beautiful portrait and then pulls out the scroll from within the casket and reads what is written:

You that choose not by the view,
Chance as fair and choose as true!
Since this fortune falls to you,
Be content and seek no new.
If you be well pleased with this,
And hold your fortune for your bliss,
Turn to where your lady is
And claim her with a loving kiss.

Bassanio kisses Portia and says that the note in the casket has declared her to be his prize. This is greeted by loud applause and shouts of joy. Bassanio cannot quite believe his good fortune.

Portia tells Bassanio that for his sake she would like to

be a thousand times more fair, and ten thousand times more rich, so that she could appear more worthy in his eyes. For, she confesses, she is essentially an untutored girl, who has never attended school. She is happy that she is still young and intelligent enough to acquire knowledge and wants her gentle spirit to be directed by Bassanio. She happily declares that whatever belongs to her is now his. 'Myself and what is mine to you and yours is now converted.' Her mansion, servants and she herself are all his, she says happily.

But there is one last thing Portia would like to give Bassanio. A ring. A ring that comes with a warning. 'Which when you part from, lose or give away, will signal the end of your love,' she warns.

Bassanio is left speechless by her words, and tells Portia that he will never remove the ring from his finger, because when it leaves his finger, life will leave his body and he will be dead!

Nerissa reminds all the lords and ladies gathered there that it is time to wish the couple well. 'Let us wish them well. Good joy, my lord and lady!' Gratiano also wishes them and expresses the hope that he too would be married soon. When Bassanio wishes him luck in finding himself a wife, Gratiano reveals his fondness for Portia's maid, Nerissa, saying, 'You saw the mistress, while I beheld the maid.' So not only do the caskets decide Bassanio's fate; in a way they decide his too. Nerissa too confirms her love for Gratiano.

Bassanio proclaims happily that they would be delighted to honour their marriage at the feast.

The happy couples are soon joined by Lorenzo, Jessica and Salerio. Salerio gives Bassanio a letter from Antonio. Before opening the letter Bassanio asks about his friend, Antonio Salerio replies that 'he is neither well, nor sick and that his letter will tell of his state.'

As Bassanio reads Antonio's letter, he becomes increasingly agitated and pale. Portia fears that the letter contains bad news. Bassanio confirms that the letter does indeed bring terrible news. He confesses to Portia that when he first professed his love for her, he had claimed that he had his own money and that he was a gentleman, but in fact he had been bragging about wealth that he did not own. What he had was a loan that his friend had arranged from an enemy. And the paper contains news that his friend's ships are lost at sea and that his ventures have failed. The vessels, variously from Tripolis, Mexico, England, Lisbon, Barbary and India, have all capsized at sea.

But far worse than the fate of the ships at sea, is Shylock, the Jew. Adamant and uncompromising, Shylock reminds Antonio day and night that he has to repay the loan and accuses the state of harming trade if they deny him justice. So far twenty merchants, Antonio himself and the highest-ranking Venetian nobles have all tried to persuade him to forget his contract. But Shylock is determined to get the penalty specified in it.

Jessica claims that she had heard her father, Shylock, swear to Tubal and Chus, his countrymen, that he would rather have Antonio's flesh than twenty times the money that Antonio owes him. Antonio is in trouble indeed, she adds despairingly. Portia asks if it is Bassanio's dear friend who is in trouble. 'Yes,' says Bassanio, 'the dearest friend to me, the kindest man, the most honourable man in Italy, my friend Antonio.'

When Bassanio reveals that Antonio owes Shylock three thousand ducats on account of him, Portia suggests that he pay him back double or even triple the amount, for a friend of such sort should not have to lose even a hair due to Bassanio's fault. Portia suggests that they marry without any delay so Bassanio can then proceed to Venice to help his friend. She is willing to give him gold worth twenty times the loan so he can repay Shylock and bring Antonio back with him to Belmont.

On Portia's request, Bassanio reads Antonio's letter:

Sweet Bassanio,

My ships have all miscarried, my creditors grow cruel, my estate is very low, my bond to the Jew is forfeit; and since, in paying it, it is impossible I should live, all debts are cleared between you and me. I only wish to see you before I die. But if your love for me does not compel you to visit me, do not let this letter force you either.

Portia is shocked to hear of Antonio's troubles on account of the loan he has obtained for Bassanio and asks Bassanio to leave for Venice at once. Bassanio assures her that he will return as soon as possible and swears to remain loyal to her love.

***

Back in Venice, Shylock, in no mood for mercy, escorts Antonio to prison. Antonio tries in vain to appeal to his good sense but Shylock stays firm. He shouts mercilessly, 'I have sworn an oath that I will have my bond.' He is confident that the duke will grant him justice. Shylock repeats that he is unlikely to be swayed by any sort of appeal from a Christian man. He leaves their presence, saying, 'I'll have no speaking, I will have my bond.'

Antonio decides not to pursue Shylock any more or ply him with prayers. He feels Shylock would rather see Antonio dead, because he has often helped the people who failed to repay loans to the moneylender. Antonio does not think even the duke will bend the law in his case. Antonio believes that Venice, being a wealthy trading city, has a reputation for upholding the law, and if the duke breaks that law, its economy is likely to suffer. His cruel creditor, Shylock, will extract a pound of his flesh, he adds, and as Salarino departs, Antonio prays desperately that Bassanio would come soon to see him pay his debt; for he did not care for anything else.

***

Meanwhile, at Portia's house in Belmont, Lorenzo praises Portia for helping Antonio and tells her that Antonio is worthy of the help she has sent for him. Portia replies that she has never regretted doing a good deed, and she would not deny help to someone so close to Bassanio, for good men most often keep the company of men of similar character, and thus saving Antonio was like saving Bassanio.

Portia informs Lorenzo that she and Nerissa are moving to a monastery so she can spend her time in prayer and contemplation till Bassanio returns. She asks Lorenzo and Jessica to look after the estate in her absence. She believes that her people will accept them in place of herself and Bassanio, and bids them goodbye. She then asks her servant Balthazar to go to Padua to deliver a letter to her cousin, Doctor Bellario. Doctor Bellario in turn would give Balthazar certain documents and clothing for Portia. Balthazar on his part must take these and proceed quickly by ferry to Venice where Portia and Nerissa would meet him.

Portia has been laying her plans carefully. But Nerissa is perplexed when Portia whispers to her that they are going to Venice to meet their new husbands dressed as young men. 'I'll be the prettier fellow of the two … and speak with a reedy voice and turn my steps into a manly stride,' she jests merrily. Urging Nerissa to hurry, as a coach already awaits them at the gate of the park, she promises to explain everything when they are in the coach enroute to Venice.

***

Once Portia and Nerissa depart for the monastery, Launcelot Gobbo and Jessica take a stroll in a garden in Belmont. Launcelot tells Jessica that he fears that she will suffer damnation on account of her father, as there is truth in the saying that the sins of the father shall be delivered upon the children. But Jessica insists that marrying Lorenzo has been her salvation as she is now a Christian. Launcelot argues that by converting Jews, who do not eat pork, to Christians, one is only effectively raising the price of pork! The exasperated Jessica threatens to tell her husband what Launcelot has been telling her.

They are joined by Lorenzo a short while later. When Launcelot finally leaves them alone and goes in to check if dinner has been laid, he says wearily, 'The fool has planted in his memory an army of good words.' Lorenzo then asks Jessica what she thinks of Lord Bassanio's wife. Jessica answers that Portia is matchless; there is no one quite like her and that Bassanio is indeed blessed to have got such a remarkable wife. Lorenzo says that he is as good a husband to Jessica as Portia is a wife to Bassanio. Jessica teasingly says that he needs to consult her on that, as they get ready to eat dinner.

4

The day of judgement finally dawns. Everyone is gathered at the Court of Justice. The Duke of Venice, the wealthy nobles, Antonio, Bassanio, Gratiano, Salarino, Solanio and others. The duke heralds the start of proceedings. 'What, is Antonio here?'

'Ready, so please your grace,' Antonio says in reply. The duke expresses his regret at the kind of adversary Antonio is up against. 'An inhuman wretch, incapable of pity, with no mercy in his heart,' he says of Shylock without mincing any words. Antonio says resignedly that he is ready to accept his fate.

Shylock is then summoned to court. The duke tells Shylock that he had expected him to show mercy towards Antonio, but he has been proved otherwise as Shylock seems to be determined to extract the penalty from Antonio for not paying back the loan on time. 'Which is a pound of this poor merchant's flesh,' the duke declares. A hush descends on the courtroom, as those gathered there understand the full import of such a penalty. Not only has Shylock not shown any mercy—the duke continues—but he has also thoughtlessly pursued a man who had suffered huge losses. And all this while everyone expected a gentle answer from him and some relief.

But Shylock stands firm. 'And by our holy Sabbath have I sworn to have the due and forfeit of my bond,' he says stubbornly. And he refuses to explain why he would prefer to have a pound of Antonio's flesh to three thousand ducats. 'It is my humour,' he claims. His intense feeling of hatred for Antonio is behind his passion to extract his dues. 'So I can give no reason more than a lodged hate and a certain loathing I bear Antonio, and this is why I have pursued him now that the bond is forfeit.'

Bassanio counters this logic by demanding to know, 'Do all men kill the things they do not love?'

'Does any man hate the thing he would not kill?' asks Shylock in reply.

Antonio remarks that arguing with the Jew is a pointless exercise, as there is nothing harder and more impossible to do than to try to soften a Jewish heart. He therefore appeals to them to not try to make Shylock change his mind, but to let him receive his judgement swiftly so Shylock can get what he wants.

Even when Bassanio offers Shylock six thousand ducats instead of three, he remains unmoved. He says that it doesn't matter to him how high the sum is. All he wants now is the bond—nothing less, nothing more. He then explains to the duke that as he has done no wrong, he expects no judgement.

Continuing his argument, Shylock says that just as the duke has in his service many slaves that he has purchased, whom he employs for whatever job he pleases, in the same way, the pound of flesh that he demands is his, since he has bought it, which makes it his possession. And if he is denied what is rightfully his then the rule of law in the city of Venice would have been undermined and there would no longer be any force in its orders. After Shylock finishes his argument, the duke declares that if the learned doctor, Bellario, whom he has summoned to court does not join them soon, he would dismiss the court's proceedings for the day. Just then Salerio announces that a messenger has arrived from Padua with letters from the doctor. Bassanio is relieved to hear this and says that there is still hope for Antonio. 'I will let Shylock take my flesh, blood, and bones, but not let you lose a single drop of blood,' he says to his friend.

But the dejected Antonio is resigned to his fate and says sadly that Bassanio should consider himself fortunate that he will remain alive to be able to write Antonio's epitaph. Even as he says this, Nerissa enters the court dressed like a lawyer's clerk. Nerissa greets the duke on behalf of Bellario and hands him a letter.

Meanwhile, Bassanio notices that Shylock is readying his

knife. 'Why do you whet that knife so earnestly?' he asks the Jew. To which Shylock replies, 'To cut the forfeiture from that bankrupt there.'

The duke finishes reading the letter and asks Nerissa where Doctor Bellario is. Nerissa replies that he is waiting for permission to come to the court. The duke orders some people to escort the doctor to court. In the meantime he asks a clerk to read out Bellario's letter.

Your grace, when your messenger brought me your letter I was very sick. With me at that time was a young doctor of Rome named Balthazar. I discussed the current controversy of Shylock the Jew, and Antonio the merchant, with him. We studied books and came to some wise conclusions, which were greatly aided by his knowledge. He therefore comes in place of me to perform my role at court. I appeal to you not to misjudge him on account of his youth for his is a young body with a wise head. May the trial benefit from his presence.

A few minutes later, Portia disguised as Doctor Balthazar enters the court. The duke welcomes the doctor and asks if he is familiar with the case that is currently being debated in the court. Both Antonio and Shylock step forward when the doctor asks for them to be identified. The doctor then says that the case is truly a unique one, for Shylock's argument cannot be seen as false under Venetian law even though the nature of the case is so outrageous.

When Antonio confesses to the bond, the doctor says that the only recourse left is for Shylock to be merciful. The doctor appeals to Shylock that mercy is like rain that drops from heaven, it blesses both the giver and the receiver. And he adds that if Shylock does not relent and show mercy, then the court of Venice will indeed have to pass a sentence against Antonio.

Shylock remains unrelenting. 'My deeds upon my head! I crave the law, the penalty and forfeit of my bond,' he says stubbornly. When the doctor asks if Antonio is incapable of paying back the loan, Bassanio answers that he is willing to pay ten times the sum on his friend's behalf.

The doctor states somewhat sadly that there is no power in Venice that can alter a decree for if such an example were to be set there would be many more such attempts to bend the law. Shylock is pleased with these wise pronouncements, and cheers the doctor on by saying, 'A Daniel come to judgement! Yea, a Daniel—O wise young judge, how I do honour you!' When the doctor demands to see the bond, Shylock presents it with a flourish. The doctor asks again why Shylock is unwilling to accept even three times the sum of money owed to him. In reply Shylock only reiterates his demand, 'An oath, an oath, I have an oath in heaven.'

The doctor examines the bond, and exclaims that the Jew is justified in his demand and that lawfully he may claim a pound of flesh from Antonio. In the face of the harsh penalty that the bond entails, he again begs that Shylock show mercy towards Antonio so he can tear and nullify the bond.

But Shylock, as unrelenting and unforgiving as before, presses the doctor to pass judgement and display the same good sense he has shown thus far. Antonio too appeals to the court to pass judgement without further ado. The doctor pronounces the judgement reluctantly. 'You must prepare your chest for his knife.'

Shylock is delighted to hear the judgement. As everyone in the court looks on aghast, the doctor commands that Antonio lay bare his chest. But Shylock intervenes to say that he must not bare his chest, but the place closest to the heart, for the bond states as much. The doctor asks if there is a weighing scale available at the court so the flesh can be weighed. It is after all a pound that needs to be taken—no more, no less. Shylock produces the scales without delay.

The doctor then demands to know if Shylock has with him a doctor too, as Antonio might bleed to death once a pound of flesh has been removed from his body. Shylock insists that the bond says nothing to this effect. When asked if he has anything to say, Antonio replies that he is ready to suffer the penalty and would rather die than live a life of poverty. He bids Bassanio farewell and asks him to commend him to his wife and tell her of his sad end. He also asks Bassanio to tell her that Antonio was as true a friend to Bassanio as he was to him and when Shylock cuts deep into his heart he would pay his debt for this friendship.

In reply to Antonio's heartfelt words, Bassanio says that he is married to a wife, who is as dear to him as life itself, but it is Antonio that he holds in the highest esteem. 'I would gladly lose all, sacrifice everything I have here to this devil, in order to deliver you.' The doctor remarks softly that his wife would be none too pleased to hear his offer!

Not one to remain silent, Gratiano too adds that although he has a wife who he loves dearly, he would be happy if she were dead and in heaven so she could alter the situation in the court and make the Jew change his mind. Nerissa, as the doctor's clerk sardonically says that it is good this offer has been made behind his wife's back! On hearing this talk of Christian husbands, Shylock interjects to say that he wishes his daughter had married a Jew rather than a Christian. He then requests that the judgement be passed without any further delay.

The doctor pronounces the judgement again. 'A pound of that same merchant's flesh is yours: the court awards it, and the law does allow it.' The doctor gives Shylock precise directions on how he may extract the penalty. 'And you must cut this flesh from off his breast, but in so doing not a drop of blood must be shed as this bond does give you here no jot of blood,' he tells Shylock. The bond states that the penalty is a pound of flesh alone, so it does not entitle him to take anything else, blood included.

The doctor further pronounces that if in the cutting of the flesh he sheds even one drop of blood he will have to forego his lands and his wealth, which will be confiscated by the state of Venice in accordance with the law. This will be abided to strongly—he affirms—for if Shylock demands that justice be done, justice shall indeed be done.

Shylock tries to retract by saying quickly that he is willing to take the money instead of the flesh. He says that three times the amount that is owed to him should be good enough. Bassanio quickly offers him the money.

But the doctor stops him. 'The Jew shall have justice ... he shall have nothing but the penalty,' he insists.

Then turning to Shylock he instructs him to cut off Antonio's flesh but without shedding a drop of blood. 'Prepare to cut off the flesh, shed no blood, nor cut less, nor more, but just a pound of flesh.' For if Shylock takes more, or less than a pound, equal in excess of as little as the weight of a hair, then he will be sentenced to death and his wealth will be confiscated.

Seeing Shylock hesitate, the doctor eggs him on. 'Why does the Jew pause? Take your forfeiture,' he says encouragingly. Shylock, getting more agitated by the minute, now asks only for the principal amount and nothing more. 'Give me my principal, and let me go,' he pleads. Bassanio again offers him the money. But the doctor insists that since he had earlier refused to take the money when it was offered to him, now he shall have only justice, and his bond.

Fearing for his life, Shylock appeals again. 'Shall I not have barely my principal?'

The doctor replies, 'You shall have nothing but the forfeiture, to be so taken at your peril, Jew.'

Shylock tries to depart quickly saying, 'Why, then the devil give him good of it!'

But the doctor stops him saying that there is yet another unexplored angle to this case. Something that has been enacted in the laws of Venice: if a man seeks to take the life of another, through direct or indirect means he is liable to be charged, and the person he is trying thus to eliminate shall receive half of his wealth as compensation, while the other half will go to the state treasury. And it is for the duke to decide if such a man should live or die.

The doctor tells Shylock that he stands guilty on all counts, for he has planned Antonio's death both directly and indirectly. He asks him to beg the duke for mercy.

The duke intervenes at this point to say that he pardons Shylock his life even before he asks to show mercy, but his wealth will be divided equally, with half going to Antonio and the other half to the state. But when Shylock cries that he would rather lose his life than live without his wealth and his house, the doctor asks Antonio if he would like to show some mercy towards Shylock. In reply, Antonio says that he would like one half of Shylock's goods to become his and the other to remain with Shylock to be passed on after his death to his daughter and Lorenzo, the man who she ran away with recently. He demands that Shylock do two things—first become a Christian and second, leave his wealth and property to Lorenzo and his daughter.

The duke affirms all of Antonio's demands, and warns that if Shylock fails to follow these, he will revoke the pardon he has granted Shylock. Shylock agrees to all the terms and conditions and asks for leave from the court, saying that he accepts the judgement. He asks that the deed be sent to him later so he can sign it.

The court adjourns soon after. The duke invites Doctor Balthazar to dinner. But he declines the invitation saying that he needs to make his way back to Padua. The duke then instructs Antonio to pay the doctor as it is he who had turned the judgement in his favour. The duke then leaves the court along with his followers and the wealthy nobles of Venice.

Bassanio addresses the doctor to express his gratitude. 'Most worthy gentleman, it is because of your wisdom that my friend and I have escaped severe penalties, and in return for your services we would like to give you the three thousand ducats that we were due to pay Shylock.' But the doctor declines the offer and says that his satisfaction at having carried the proceedings to their rightful conclusion is payment enough. He takes their leave with the mysterious comment, 'I pray you, know me when we meet again: I wish you well.'

But Bassanio insists that he take with him something, not as a fee but to remember them by. The disguised doctor asks Antonio for his gloves and Bassanio for his ring. 'Give me your gloves, I'll wear them for your sake,' he says to Antonio. And to Bassanio he says, 'And, for your love, I'll take this ring from you.' In reply Bassanio makes an excuse, remembering his promise to Portia, and says to the doctor, 'This ring, good sir? Alas, it is a worthless item; I will not shame myself by giving you this.' But the doctor is adamant. 'I will have nothing else but only this; and now I feel I really want it.'

The hapless Bassanio, unwilling to part with the ring Portia had given him, offers other rings instead. 'The dearest ring in Venice will I give you … only for this, I pray you, pardon me.' When the doctor questions him further, Bassanio explains, 'Good sir, this ring was given me by my wife; and, when she put it on, she made me vow that I should neither sell, nor give, nor lose it.' The doctor remains unmoved and says that his wife does not know how much the doctor deserves the ring! Saying this, the doctor and the clerk also leave the court.

Antonio then asks Bassanio to give the doctor the ring so he can demonstrate that the debt they owe him is more valuable than his wife's instruction. Bassanio instructs Gratiano to give the doctor the ring and bring him back to Antonio's house. Bassanio and Antonio also leave the court for Antonio's house. They plan to leave for Belmont in the morning.

***

Still dressed as the doctor and the clerk, Portia and Nerissa make their way slowly along a street in Venice. Portia tells Nerissa to find Shylock's house and give him the deed to sign, so that they can then leave for Belmont and reach there before their husbands return. Portia feels that Lorenzo will certainly welcome the deed that makes him heir to half of Shylock's wealth.

As they are walking along, Gratiano suddenly catches up with them and gives the doctor the ring that Bassanio has sent for him. He also extends Bassanio's invitation for dinner that night.

The doctor declines the dinner invitation, but happily accepts the ring. He then requests Gratiano to show the clerk the way to Shylock's house.

Nerissa whispers to Portia as she leaves, 'I'll see if I can get my husband's ring, which I did make him swear to keep forever.' Portia replies, 'they will protest and swear that they did indeed give the rings to men, but we will outswear them.' She asks Nerissa to hurry back.

5

As Lorenzo and Jessica walk along the road that leads to Portia's house in Belmont, Portia's servant, Stephano, informs them that Portia will be back at Belmont before sunrise as she is presently at the holy crosses, praying for a blissful wedded life. Launcelot also announces the arrival of his master, Bassanio, the following morning.

When Portia and Nerissa reach home a short while later and find that Bassanio and Gratiano are not yet back, Portia asks Nerissa to instruct the servants not to reveal that they had been out of the house. She also tells Lorenzo and Jessica not to divulge anything.

Even as Portia and Nerissa are giving instructions, a trumpet announces the arrival of Bassanio, Antonio, Gratiano and their followers.

'You are welcome home, my lord,' Portia says to Bassanio as he enters the house. Bassanio introduces Antonio to her, 'This is the man, this is Antonio, to whom I am so infinitely bound.' To which Portia replies that he should indeed be bound to Antonio for Antonio was much bound to him.

Gratiano and Nerissa meanwhile have already got into an argument. Nerissa is questioning Gratiano on the whereabouts of the ring she had given him before he left. Gratiano claims that he had given it to the judge's clerk, a little boy, who had begged to have it as a fee.

'No, God's my judge, the clerk will never wear hair on his face that had it.' Nerissa angrily suspects that Gratiano has given the ring to a woman.

'He will and if he live to be a man,' Gratiano replies.

'Ay, if a woman live to be a man,' Nerissa argues.

Portia intervenes to rebuke Gratiano for giving away the first gift that his wife had given him. She says that she too had given her husband Bassanio a ring, and told him never to part with it. On hearing this, Bassanio wishes he could cut his left hand off, as he too, like Gratiano, was no longer in possession of the ring that Portia had given him. Gratiano then reveals that Bassanio had given away his ring to the judge who had begged to have it. Just like the judge's clerk had begged to have Gratiano's ring.

Portia then turns on Bassanio and says, 'What ring did you give away, my lord? I hope it was not the one you received of me.' But Bassanio has no ring to show. Portia and Nerissa are enraged and say they will not be satisfied till they see their rings again.

'If you only knew to whom I gave the ring, and for what I gave the ring, and how unwillingly I left the ring, because nothing else was acceptable but the ring, you would not be so displeased,' Bassanio argues.

'If you had known the virtue of the ring, or half her worthiness who gave the ring, or your own honour to contain the ring, you would not have parted with the ring,' Portia counters. Bassanio could have resisted if he had the will, she continues, accusing him of having actually given it to a woman.

'No, by mine honour, madam, I gave it to no woman but a civil doctor, who refused the three thousand ducats, and begged for the ring instead … and had you been there you would have begged me to give the ring to the doctor too,' Bassanio argues.

But Portia pretends to remain unmoved. 'Do not let that doctor come near my house, as he has the jewel I love.'

Nerissa also adds that she too will have the clerk, instead of Gratiano!

Antonio, meanwhile, hopelessly stuck between the star-crossed lovers, says that he is the unhappy subject of these quarrels. He tries to argue Bassanio's case by saying that he did once lend Bassanio money and were it not for the man who Bassanio gave the ring to, he had very nearly lost the case. And even as Bassanio asks for forgiveness and promises never again to break an oath, Portia tells Antonio to be his guarantor and gives him a ring to give to Bassanio. Antonio gives the ring to Bassanio with the words, 'Here, Lord Bassanio; swear to keep this ring.' Bassanio jumps when he sees the ring and cries out, 'By heaven! It is the same I gave the doctor.'

To bring an end to the confusion, Portia produces a letter from Bellario in Padua, wherein it states that Portia was the doctor and Nerissa her clerk. She says Lorenzo is witness to the fact that she had left Belmont after Bassanio did and had only now returned.

Then addressing Antonio, Portia says that she has excellent news for him. The letter also states that three of Antonio's ships are back in harbour, safe and sound. Antonio is dumbfounded on hearing this news.

Bassanio cannot restrain himself any longer. He asks, 'Were you the doctor, and did you have me fooled?'

'Were you the clerk?' Gratiano quickly asks Nerissa.

Antonio thanks Portia for giving him the good news that his ships are safely at harbour. Nerissa gives Lorenzo the deed—signed by Shylock—which states that after his death all his wealth will belong to Lorenzo and Jessica. Lorenzo is delighted to hear this.

As the warring couples are finally at peace, Gratiano, the man with more words than any other man in Venice, has the last one here too. 'Well, while I live, I'll fear no other thing so much as keeping safe Nerissa's ring.'

Supplementary Reading

Character Sketches

SHYLOCK

Shylock, a Jewish moneylender, is clearly the most hated person in *The Merchant of Venice*, and one of Shakespeare's strongest characterisations. His character has given rise to both debate and criticism. In purely simplistic terms, Shylock is the stereotypical miserly Jewish man who epitomises some of man's biggest vices—greed, revengefulness, and lack of compassion. It matters less that he has lost his daughter when she runs away with Lorenzo, and more that she has taken with her his precious jewels. And his intense hatred of Christians translates into a strong desire to seek revenge on Antonio and nothing and no one can sway him from his resolve, not even twenty merchants and the highest-ranking Venetian nobles.

But, it remains debatable whether Shylock is truly the villain or whether he is considered one because of his faith. Throughout the play his evilness is associated with his faith and there is a clear implication that his salvation lies in his becoming a Christian. But does his dislike and hatred of Christians arise out of the resentment Jews feel on account of centuries of persecution at the hands of society? These are important questions that the play raises.

In possibly the most powerful speech in the play, Shylock asks that do Jews not have hands, organs, dimensions, senses, affections and passions like any other man? "If you prick us, do we not bleed? If you tickle us, do we not laugh? If you poison us, do we not die? And if you wrong us, shall we not revenge?" While this draws no sympathy from those it addresses, as readers we are compelled to dwell on these pertinent questions.

Shylock's most abiding characteristic remains his adamant and uncompromising behaviour. He pursues the bankrupt Antonio day and night to repay the loan and accuses the state of harming trade if they deny him justice. He accuses Antonio of disrupting his business at the Rialto by lending money, without too much emphasis on surety or guarantee. He feels that Antonio has disgraced and obstructed his business and dealings a great many times, mocked his losses, interfered or foreclosed his bargains. And all because he is a Jew.

And in the end Shylock exits a defeated and embittered man. He loses his wealth, half to Antonio and half to his daughter Jessica, and son-in-law, Lorenzo, to be given to them on his death. So while it appears that justice has been brought, the beliefs it is based on remain debatable.

ANTONIO

Despite being the central character of this play, Antonio's character is problematic in that his view of Shylock's villainy is clouded by his belief in the evilness of all Jews. In fact all of Antonio's virtues such as kindness, benevolence and love amount to his being a good Christian, just like all of Shylock's negative qualities amount to his being a bad Jew. Whether Shakespeare intended to portray Antonio and Shylock in clear roles of protagonist and villain to show up the contrast of good versus evil is again debatable. As is the danger of labelling either faith good or bad, even though they are clearly pitted against each other all through the play. In fact for Antonio to suggest that Shylock convert to Christianity as a solution to his innate evil, (and by implication) Jewish nature calls for criticism and debate.

But what we do have is a kind and honourable man, even if somewhat lacklustre, kinder than any other man in Venice and more honourable than most. And in the strongest contrast to Shylock, a man who does not seek revenge and shows mercy towards Shylock when the judgement pronounces that he must give away all his wealth.

And he is a man with a heart. A man who values friendship over all else. For even though his business is precarious and his merchant vessels are out at sea, he is willing to take the risk of borrowing money for his friend, Bassanio. And when Shylock announces the cruel stipulation that he will lose a pound of flesh if he forfeits the bond, Antonio is willing even to risk his life for his friend.

In fact, so dear is his friendship and so strong his love for Bassanio, that he cares not for his troubles, but wants only that Bassanio should think chiefly of the courtship and later when he incurs huge losses at sea and is very nearly bankrupt can only think of his obligation to his friend, Bassanio.

This then is Antonio, the man Bassanio considers his dearest friend, the kindest man … the most honourable man in Italy. But is it his innate goodness that turns the case in his favour in the end and Shylock's inherent villainy that brings him to justice? Those are some more questions that this play raises and to which there are no clear answers.

BASSANIO

In Bassanio—a Venetian scholar and soldier—are captured all the qualities that make for a good friend, undying loyalty and unquestioning love for Antonio, a man he is willing to give his life for. He is also unwavering in his love for Portia. And the play takes off from his desire to be suitor to Portia. Bassanio loves Antonio to death, and he also loves Portia, he loves masques, being with friends, jesting with friends, courting Portia. And he does all this with a passion. In the end he is the most suitable man for Portia and clearly the luckiest as he makes the wisest choice in the caskets. He goes for the plainest of the three and wins the lottery of the caskets and Portia's hand.

It is to Bassanio's credit that Antonio is unwavering in his loyalty towards him. But unlike Antonio, Bassanio is suspicious of Shylock's intentions and does not want Antonio to agree to the moneylender's terms. And so it is that when he learns of Antonio's troubles at Belmont, his concern almost borders on guilt and in court he tries everything he can do to avert the verdict he feels Antonio will be faced with. He claims that he would lose all, sacrifice everything to the devil to be able to deliver him from this judgement. He offers up to ten times the borrowed amount to Shylock, if he would only show mercy towards his friend.

In the end, Bassanio is the happiest. Antonio has emerged unharmed from court and Bassanio has won Portia forever, in spite of the brief dispute over the travelling ring.

PORTIA

Portia, the beautiful heiress of Belmont, described simply as a woman of wonderful virtues, proves to be just this—a wise and wonderful woman of virtues, and one of Shakespeare's strongest women characters. Courted by some suitable, and mostly unsuitable suitors, Portia is unwilling to disregard her father's arrangement of the lottery of the caskets, saying she would rather remain unwed if her hand were not won in the way her father had wished for. And she remains fair, assuring the dark-complexioned Prince of Morocco that appearance does not sway her since the lottery gives everyone a fair chance.

When Bassanio wins the lottery and her hand, she makes a very honest confession about being an untutored girl, but this very woman who has not received any formal education turns the case at court. It is Portia (disguised as Doctor Balthazar) who truly saves Antonio. It is her clever and careful study of the bond and her knowledge of Venetian laws that prevents Shylock from taking a pound of Antonio's flesh, thereby saving the latter's life.

And this is not the only instance in which she shows her good sense. On seeing how agitated Bassanio gets on hearing of Antonio's misfortune, it is Portia who urges him to save his friend by paying even three times the amount Antonio owes Shylock. She trusts that Antonio is likely to be as good a man as Bassanio is for men keep the company of those like themselves.

As Bassanio's wife, she is inflexible in her loyalty. But, that apart, Portia has a good plan in place, when she dresses up as a young man along with her waiting maid, Nerissa, and travels to Venice, where she successfully turns the case and relieves Antonio from blame.

And in the end she is a happy woman, for she seems to have brought about order again—because of her convincing disguise, and her cleverness at court and elsewhere, Bassanio's friend is saved from harm and she finds in Bassanio a suitable husband.

Questions

1

a. Who is Antonio and what does his friend Bassanio tell him?
b. What are Portia and her waiting maid Nerissa discussing?
c. What is the lottery of the three caskets? Who devised it and for whom?
d. Describe any one suitor who has tried unsuccessfully to win Portia's hand.
e. Who is Shylock and what does Bassanio want from him?
f. What practices of Shylock as a moneylender does Antonio disapprove of?
g. What are the terms of the bond that Antonio enters into with Shylock?

2

a. What do Launcelot Gobbo and Old Gobbo want from Bassanio?
b. Who is Jessica and what is she planning to do?
c. Name the persons who help Jessica escape from her father's house.

d. What do the three caskets proclaim? Which casket does the Prince of Morocco choose?
e. What are the three things a suitor must swear to before choosing a casket?

3

a. What is being rumoured at the Rialto?
b. Who is Tubal and what is the task that Shylock has given him?
c. What happens when Bassanio chooses the casket?
d. Why does Portia give Bassanio a ring? And what does she warn him not to do?
e. Why does Antonio send a letter to Bassanio and what does the letter say?
f. What does Shylock want from Antonio after he fails to follow the terms of the bond?
g. What do Portia and Nerissa plan to do?

4

a. Who are the people at court and why are they gathered there?
b. Why does Shylock not show mercy towards Antonio? What are the reasons he gives?
c. Who are Doctor Balthazar and the clerk and why do

they come to the court dressed as young men?

d. What judgement does the doctor pronounce on Antonio? What does he ask Shylock to do?
e. How is the case turned around at court? What is the judge's verdict?
f. What is Shylock accused of having done under Venetian law?
g. What does Antonio ask Shylock to do to make up for endangering Antonio's life?
h. Why do both the doctor and the clerk demand the rings from Bassanio and Gratiano?

5

a. Why is Nerissa, dressed as the judge's clerk, going in search of Shylock?
b. What secret does Portia not want the servants to reveal to Bassanio?
c. Where are Bassanio and Gratiano's rings and why are Portia and Nerissa angry?
d. Whose ring does Portia ask Antonio to give to Bassanio?
e. What news does the letter from Bellario contain? And what news does Portia give to Antonio?

About Shakespeare and his Plays

WHO WAS SHAKESPEARE?

William Shakespeare (1564-1616) was an English poet and playwright. He is now widely regarded as the greatest writer in the English language and the greatest playwright of all time.

Shakespeare was baptised on 26 April 1564 in Stratford-Upon-Avon. His father John was a glovemaker and dealer in wool. His mother Mary was the daughter of a prosperous farmer. They had eight children.

In 1582, Shakespeare married Anne Hathaway. They had three children, Susanna, Hamnet and Judith.

Little is known about Shakespeare until 1592. At this time, records show that he was living in London and writing poetry. His early plays were also written during this period.

In 1592, Shakespeare became a founding member, actor and playwright of the Lord Chamberlain's Men, a theatre company. The most famous actor in this company was Richard Burbage, who played the roles of characters like Richard III, Othello and Lear. This company was later renamed the King's Men.

Little else is known about Shakespeare's life, though he clearly earned a lot of money for his plays. He became a substantial landowner.

He died in 1616, and was buried in Stratford.

In 1623, two actors from the King's Men had Shakespeare's plays published in what is now called the *First Folio.* This contained thirty-six plays and was sold for £1.

The period during which Shakespeare lived and wrote is now called the Elizabethan age, during the reign of Queen Elizabeth I (1533-1603), during which many great playwrights, such as Christopher Marlowe and Ben Jonson, wrote.

The works of Shakespeare that survive include thirty-eight plays, 154 sonnets and two long narrative poems. Shakespeare's plays have been translated into every major language, read, performed on stage and made into films, and continue to inspire new interpretations all around the world even today.

WHY READ SHAKESPEARE?

'Shakespeare's work is the fullest expression of the dilemmas that we as humans face ... he's capable of seeing two sides of a situation so there's always drama and there's always conflict.'—Michael Boyd, RSC Artistic Director.

Shakespeare is still read and loved because his plays

contain fabulous stories and wonderful characters, and are full of marvellous poetry.

Shakespeare's plays are best watched first and then read, because in performance they take on a new magic. Today many filmmakers are making films on Shakespeare's plays. You can try watching them to get a sense of how the plays would be in performance.

PLAYS AND THE THEATRE IN SHAKESPEARE'S TIME

Performances in Elizabethan theatres were very different from when you go to see a play now. The actors and the audience always interacted. Shakespeare's company had to perform against the noise of the crowd which shouted, threw fruits and tried to join the actors on stage.

Unlike the playwrights of today, writers like Shakespeare would have to present their theatre company with their ideas. The leading actors and managers would decide whether they liked it or not, and only then would the playwright proceed. This close relationship meant that the playwrights often wrote roles with a particular actor in mind.

When a play was completed, actors would receive only their lines, and not the whole play. Thus, until rehearsals started, they would not have any idea how the parts would fit together to form a cohesive play. Rehearsals were used to sort out all the details not mentioned in the script, such as songs, exits and on-stage actions.

The Elizabethan stage was different from the proscenium stage we see in theatres nowadays. The cheaper tickets were for the groundlings, the audience on three sides of the stage. The more expensive tickets were for patrons who sat in covered seats further back. The stage was covered in straw. The wall at the back had three entrances. Above the stage was a trapdoor for lowering performers down to the stage, and on the stage itself was another trapdoor for surprise entrances and exits.